Carl Can Run

by Warwick Dean
illustrated by Kate Ashforth

SCHOOL PUBLISHERS

Printed in the United States of America

ISBN 10: 0-15-350359-9
ISBN 13: 978-0-15-350359-7

Ordering Options
ISBN 10: 0-15-350331-9 (Grade 1 Below-Level Collection)
ISBN 13: 978-0-15-350331-3 (Grade 1 Below-Level Collection)
ISBN 10: 0-15-357402-X (package of 5)
ISBN 13: 978-0-15-357402-3 (package of 5)

1 2 3 4 5 6 7 8 9 10   179   15 14 13 12 11 10 09 08 07 06

"Come to my house, Carl,"
said Greg.

2

Carl went with Greg.

"Let's all run," said Greg.

4

"Will you say *go*, Mom?"
asked Greg.
"Make it loud!"

The run started, but Carl
fell down.

"Put your cap on again,
Carl," said Mrs. Archer.
"Run!"

"I feel good!" said Carl.
"I know I fell, but I
finished!"